This Storybook Belongs To

Princess _____

# One True Love

ADVANCE
PUBLISHERS

"I'm baaack!" yelled the Genie. "How's my favorite couple?"

"We've missed you," said Aladdin. "How was your trip around the world?"

"Fabulous!" the Genie replied. "I saw the pyramids in Egypt, went skiing in Sweden, and worked on my tan in the Caribbean. A nice shade of blue, don't you think?"

A spark flew from the Genie's finger, and soon Aladdin and Jasmine were surrounded by gifts from every country the Genie had visited! The Genie had a special surprise for Aladdin.

"A kangaroo?" Aladdin gasped as the kangaroo leaped over the palace wall. "I'd better go catch it!"

"Be careful!" yelled the Genie. "Kangaroos know how to box!"

"Oh, Genie, it's good to have you back in Agrabah," said Jasmine. Then she noticed the Genie looked a little sad. "What's the matter?" she asked.

"All that traveling was great, but it got a bit lonely," he began. "I wish I could find a genie to share my life with."

Jasmine put her hand on his shoulder. "I know how that can feel," she said. "Remember...I went through a lot of suitors before I found my one true love."

Jasmine began to tell the Genie her story. "I told my father that I wanted to marry for love," Jasmine explained. "But the law stated that I had to marry a prince. No matter what I said, my father didn't listen to me. He summoned every suitor he could to come and court me."

"Sounds like you were pretty popular!" the Genie interjected.

"Popular? Yes. Happy? No!" said Jasmine.

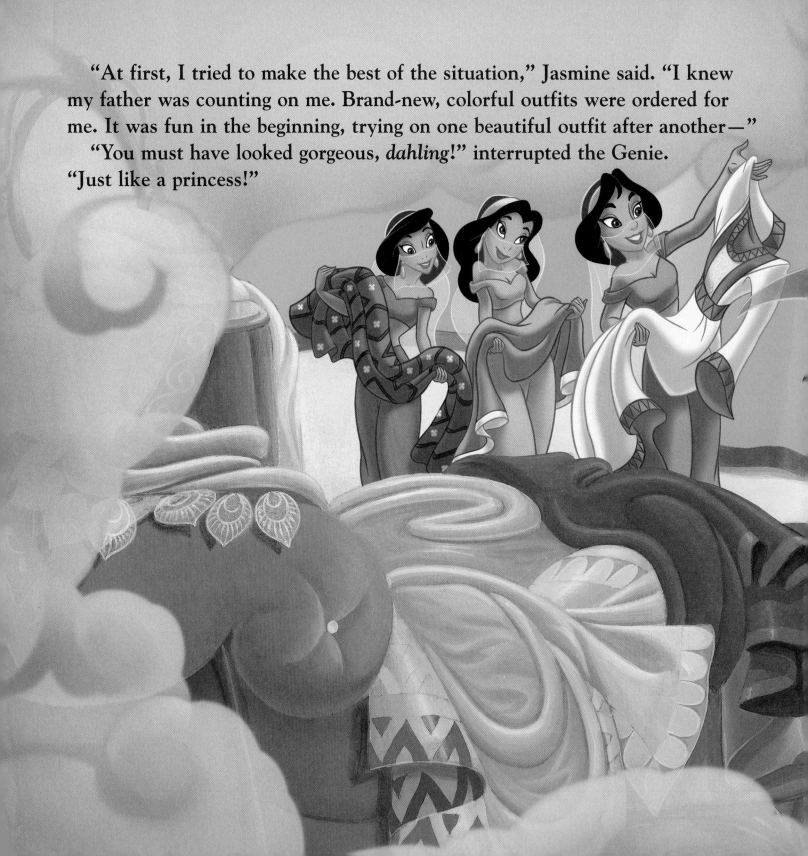

"At first, I tried to make the best of the situation," Jasmine said. "I knew my father was counting on me. Brand-new, colorful outfits were ordered for me. It was fun in the beginning, trying on one beautiful outfit after another—"

"You must have looked gorgeous, *dahling*!" interrupted the Genie. "Just like a princess!"

"And then, of course, there were the jewels. It all seemed too good to be true...till I met the suitors." Jasmine sighed. "Soon I realized that the problem wasn't the outfits—it was the suitors!"

First there was Prince Achoo (or that's the name Jasmine remembered).

"Princess Jasmine," said the prince. "A-a-a-choo! It's so — Achoo! — nice to meet you."

Jasmine's eyes grew wide. "Are you allergic to me?" she asked.

"Achoo! Oh, no, Princess Jasmine!" said the prince. "It's not just you—it seems that I'm allergic to everything in your palace! I must go!"

As the days passed, each suitor seemed worse than the one before.

"I have a kingdom where all you'd have to worry about is the cooking and cleaning," said Prince Macho.

Jasmine was shocked. "You want me to do your chores?"

"Yes, I prefer a wife to do them," said Prince Macho.

"Oh, really? I prefer a husband who isn't living in the Stone Age!"

Next was Prince Wishy-Washy.

"So, tell me," began Jasmine, "what do you like to do?"

"Whatever you like to do, Princess," replied the prince.

"Well...what do you like to eat?" asked Jasmine.

"Whatever you eat, Princess," he replied.

Jasmine decided to have a little fun. "We're having roasted ant pitas with rat hummus for lunch. How does that sound?"

Prince Wishy-Washy didn't think it sounded very good!

Then one night, Prince Ali came to Jasmine's balcony.

"I do not want to see you," she told him. Jasmine was tired of all the suitors. She was tired of feeling like a prize to be won.

"You're right," said Prince Ali. "You aren't just some prize to be won. You should be free to make your own choice."

Soon after, Jasmine discovered that Prince Ali was Aladdin in disguise. And no laws could keep true love from blossoming....

"Genie? Genie! What's wrong?" Jasmine asked.

The Genie was bawling like a baby. "That was the sweetest story I've ever heard!"

Jasmine laughed and became a bit embarrassed. "Genie, you can find the same happiness that Aladdin and I share. I just know your special genie is out there!"

"Really?" asked the Genie.

Just then, Aladdin showed up with the kangaroo. "You were right, Genie. That kangaroo has a strong right punch," he said, holding his arm.

"No time to talk, Al," said the Genie, rushing past. "I've got a genie to find—and not a thing to wear!"

"What's with him?" Aladdin asked Jasmine.

"He wants to have what we have," replied Jasmine, kissing Aladdin on the cheek. "True love."

Within minutes the Genie reappeared. He did a quick fashion show for Jasmine and Aladdin. "Do I go for the handsome banker look? Or the tuxedo look? Or maybe the preppy, golf-playing look? Or perhaps the surfer look? Which one do you think works best?" the Genie asked.

"You want someone to like you for who you are on the inside," Jasmine said. "Just be yourself."

A light bulb went off above the Genie's head.

"Presto-change-o!" he said, and all the clothes vanished. "How do you like my new...er...old look?"

"It fits perfectly," Jasmine said warmly.

After the Genie had left, Aladdin and Jasmine went on a Magic Carpet ride. Jasmine snuggled close to Aladdin. Suddenly she saw a mountaintop covered with a blanket and food.

"Our own private picnic!" said Jasmine. "Oh, Aladdin! I'm so lucky to have you!"

Aladdin shook his head. "No, I'm the lucky one."

As they enjoyed their sunset picnic, Jasmine thought again about all those suitors she had had to go through. Because of them, she was grateful for the gift of true love that she had finally found with Aladdin.

"Well, Jasmine," said Aladdin, "it's been quite a day."

"And there's no one I'd rather end it with than you," Jasmine told him with a smile.